THE SOCCER MACHINE

Follow the Team!

DAVID BEDFORD

THE SOCCER MACHINE

Illustrated by Keith Brumpton

Kane Miller

A DIVISION OF EDC PUBLISHING

First American Edition 2006
by Kane/Miller Book Publishers, Inc.
La Jolla, California

First published in 2003 by Little Hare Books, Australia
For information contact:
Kane Miller, A Division of EDC Publishing
P.O. Box 470663
Tulsa, OK 74147-0663
www.kanemiller.com
www.edcpub.com

Library of Congress Control Number: 2005930840
Printed and bound in the United States of America
2 3 4 5 6 7 8 9 10

ISBN: 978-1-933605-00-5

To Deborah, Paeony and Pat – my teachers

DB

Chapter 1

8-0!

How could The Team lose 8-0?

"We're terrible," muttered Harvey.

"Terrible, terrible, terrible!"

The Team sat in the center circle after the game. They were covered in mud, and too tired to move.

"We're not *that* bad," said Rita, as she picked dried freckles of mud from her face.

Harvey got slowly to his feet. "We *are* that bad," he said. "And we're getting worse."

Harvey walked home in his socks,
dragging his cleats behind him. Soccer was
the only thing Harvey was good at — and he
was still terrible.

Harvey lived on Baker Street. Baker Street
was on a hill. At the top of the hill was
Harvey's house. Next door to Harvey's house
there was a tall tower shaped like a rocket,
with a window at the top.

When Harvey reached Baker Street, there was a noise like thunder.

"Haaarrveyyy!"

It sounded like an airplane was landing on his head. Harvey ducked. Then he looked up.

Professor Gertie, Harvey's neighbor, was leaning from the window. She was wearing a bright yellow mask with a long beak, like a duck with its mouth open.

"It's me!" boomed Professor Gertie's voice. "I'm wearing my Shouting Mask! I've just invented it! Did you win?"

"No!" shouted Harvey.

"Oh, rats! Come on up!"

Harvey walked slowly up the hill to the tower. He ducked inside the round door and climbed the twisting stairs. Professor Gertie was waiting for him at the top. She pulled off her Shouting Mask.

"What was the score?" Professor Gertie asked.

"8-0," said Harvey.

"Double rats!" said Professor Gertie. "The Team aren't very good, are they?"

"We're terrible," Harvey agreed.

"What about the Bouncing Boots?" Professor Gertie had glued springs to the bottom of Harvey's soccer cleats. "Did they help you jump?"

"Yes," said Harvey. "But I couldn't *stop* jumping. I knocked over Steffi and Matt. Then I bounced on Darren, I bounced on Rita, and I landed on the referee. The ref made me take my cleats off and play in my socks. And he gave me a yellow card."

"What about the Smoke Machine?"
Professor Gertie had sewn a miniature
Smoke Machine into Harvey's shorts.

Harvey turned around. There was a
large hole in the back of his shorts, with
burn marks around the edge. Through the
hole you could see Harvey's shiny red
underpants.

"The Fireproof Underpants worked!" said Professor Gertie proudly.

"I guess," said Harvey. "They got a bit hot, though."

"Was there a lot of smoke?"

"Tons," said Harvey. "I got the ball, turned on the Smoke Machine, and — whoosh! — no one could see where I was. I nearly scored! But there was so much smoke that I couldn't see the goal. Then nobody could see anything at all. The ref said I had to stop making smoke or he'd give me a red card."

"Stupid ref!" said Professor Gertie.

"He doesn't like me," said Harvey. "Not since I landed on him."

"Next week we'll show him!" cried Professor Gertie. "I'm going to invent something so brilliant that you won't be able to lose."

"I'm not wearing Fireproof Underpants again," said Harvey. "They itch."

"I've got a better idea!" said Professor Gertie. She took her pencil from behind her ear and opened her notebook. "Tell me how you play soccer."

Harvey thought for a minute. "We chase the ball," he said. "And we tackle to get the ball. Then we try to *keep* the ball …"

"What else?" asked Professor Gertie, writing a list.

Harvey scratched his head. There *was* something else. What was it? Oh, right. "We're *supposed* to score goals," Harvey said. "But we haven't done that yet."

"Tut tut!" Professor Gertie stuck her pencil in her mouth and read her list out loud.

How To Play Soccer
Chase
Tackle
Keep the ball
Score goals

"Now, which of these do you do badly?"

"All of them," said Harvey.

Later that night, something woke Harvey up.
Bang-clatter-blop noises were coming from
Professor Gertie's tower.

Suddenly, there was a flash of lightning. Then a voice Harvey had never heard before said, "Aw, shucks!" and a strange rubbery smell drifted in through his bedroom window…

Professor Gertie was making something. What could it be? And would it really be good enough to help The Team win at last?

Chapter 2

Harvey didn't see Professor Gertie all that
week. She had locked herself in her tower
and wouldn't answer the door. But on
Saturday morning, when Harvey left his
house to go to the game, he found Professor
Gertie waiting for him.

There was something waiting with her.
Something strange. Something *very* strange.

It was wearing a white soccer shirt with a large red star on it — just like Harvey. But its head looked like it was made from an old trashcan covered in pink jelly. Its nose was a plug. And its eyes were red lights, like scanners at a supermarket checkout. Harvey thought he saw one of the eyes wink at him.

"Er ... hello," Harvey said.

"He won't answer back," said Professor Gertie.

"Can't he talk?" asked Harvey.

"No," said Professor Gertie. "His brain is pure soccer. He chases. He tackles. He keeps the ball. *And* he scores goals. He's a Soccer Machine, and he's programmed to win! Watch."

Professor Gertie pressed the red star on the Soccer Machine's shirt. The Soccer Machine started stretching and jumping up and down.

"He's a bit creaky," said Harvey.

Professor Gertie took an oilcan from the pocket of her lab coat and oiled the Soccer Machine's joints.

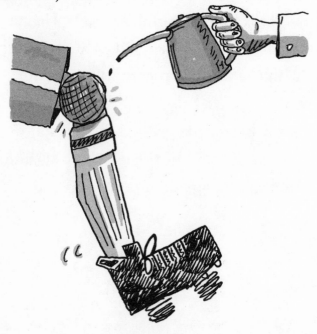

"His body is metal," she explained, "and he's covered from head to foot with Squidgy Skin. Bouncing Boots are built in, and he has a top speed of 35 miles per hour. These are Skidders, for braking. And this is a Spinner, for turning."

As the Soccer Machine demonstrated the Spinner, Harvey asked, "What's his name?"

"I call him Soccer Machine Mark 1," said Professor Gertie. "Mark 1 means that he's the first of his kind — number one."

"I'll call him Mark 1," Harvey decided.

"Good!" said Professor Gertie. "Now remember, press his button once for warm-up exercises, twice for play, and three times to turn him off."

"How do I get him to follow me to the field?"

"That's easy," said Professor Gertie. "Just hold his hand."

"No way!"

"Go on!" Professor Gertie put one of Mark 1's hands into Harvey's. It felt squidgy — and warm. "Now, off you go!"

Harvey led Mark 1 to the bottom of the hill and turned the corner out of Baker Street. When he was sure Professor Gertie couldn't see him anymore, Harvey tried to pull his hand away, but Mark 1 wouldn't let go. Harvey pulled harder, but Mark 1's grip was as strong as steel.

"I give up!" said Harvey, and Mark 1's eyes blinked.

When they got to the soccer field, everyone stared.

"Harvey?" asked Darren. "What are you *doing*?"

Harvey blushed. "This is Mark 1. He's a Soccer Machine, and he's going to help us win," he explained.

"Why are you holding his hand?" asked Rita.

"To make him follow," said Harvey.

The Team were not impressed.

Then the Ham Soccer Furies arrived. They were dressed in yellow and black, and looked like a swarm of bees. Their captain started laughing.

"Is that your star player?" he asked. "Do you have to hold his hand in case he falls over?" All the Ham players laughed.

"It's embarrassing!" whispered Darren. "Harvey's machine can't play."

"Yes he can!" said Rita angrily. "We're one short anyway, because Steffi's on vacation. And it will teach Ham a lesson if Mark 1 helps us win."

"He'll probably just get in our way," muttered Darren.

Rita said, "If he's no good, we'll take him out. Okay, Harvey?"

"Okay," said Harvey.

The Team got into position. The Ham players were still laughing as they kicked off.

Harvey pressed Mark 1's button twice for "play," then let go of his hand.

"Aw, shucks!" said Mark 1.

"He can talk!" said Rita.

"He's not supposed to," said Harvey. He thought he saw a funny look in Mark 1's eyes. Then Harvey had to chase Ham to get the ball, and he was too busy to see if Mark 1 really could play soccer or not.

At last, Harvey got the ball.

"Pass, Harvey!" his teammates called.

But Harvey couldn't see anyone to pass to, and a Ham forward took the ball from him. The Ham players cheered.

Then — *whoooom!* — something shot past Harvey so fast the wind blew his hair across his eyes. He could just make out a white shirt with a red star on it, and a pink-jelly head shaped like a trashcan.

Chapter 3

Harvey stood still and watched in amazement.

Mark 1 pounced on the ball. He dodged left. He dodged right. Then he ran straight towards the Ham goal. The Ham defenders closed in. Harvey waited for the crunching tackle but — *zzooomm!* — Mark 1 shot forward like a rocket. The Ham goalie watched him nervously. *Skid — swivel — shoot —*

"GOAL!"

Darren and Rita jumped into Harvey's arms, and they all fell over, laughing.

"He's awesome!" said Rita.

Ham kicked off. Mark 1 swooped in and took the ball. Every Ham player raced after him. But they couldn't catch him. Mark 1 swerved in and …

Goal!

Ham kicked off again. They tried to hide the ball from Mark 1 by making a circle around it. *Boing!* Mark 1 jumped inside the circle, trapped the ball between his ankles, and jumped out again. *Boing!*

The Ham goalie pulled Mark 1's shirt, but
it didn't slow Mark 1 down. He dribbled the
ball straight into the net.

Goal!

Goal! Goal! Goal!

At halftime, The Team were dancing and
cheering.

"27-0!" Shouted Rita. "I don't believe it!"

"He's beating them single-handedly!" said Darren.

But the Ham captain was shouting at the ref. "It's not fair! He's not real!"

"You weren't complaining when you first saw him!" said Rita furiously.

The ref looked Mark 1 up and down. He looked at Mark 1's Bouncing Boots and frowned. "What's your name, son?"

Mark 1's eyes flashed.

"He's a machine!" said the Ham captain. "That's why his head's like a trashcan. Harvey made him!"

"Aw, shucks!" said Mark 1. "Harveee diddle make meee!"

"What's he saying?" the ref asked Harvey. "Is he a machine?"

"Sort of," said Harvey.

The ref blew his whistle. "Game cancelled!

You can play again next week. And *you*," he
said, pointing at Harvey, "if I catch you
breaking the rules again, I'll ban you for the
rest of the season!"

The Team groaned.

"The ref's got it in for you," said Darren, "ever since you landed on him."

"I suppose it *was* cheating," said Harvey.

"Next week," said Rita, "we'll beat them fair and square."

"We're the worst team in the league," Harvey reminded her. "Next week, Ham will slaughter us."

Harvey took Mark 1's hand and led him home. Mark 1's smile seemed to have drooped. "Sorreee, Harveee," he said sadly.

"It wasn't your fault," said Harvey. Then he remembered. "Hey! You *can* talk, can't you? Go on, say something else. Say 'The Team are garbage.'"

But Mark 1 said nothing. The lights in his eyes had gone out.

Chapter 4

"What happened?"

Professor Gertie was leaning from her window, wearing her Shouting Mask. Harvey was too depressed and too tired to answer, and he let Mark 1 carry him up the twisting stairs.

Professor Gertie was bouncing up and down at the top. "You won!" she said. "I knew you would. **THE TEAM! THE TEAM! WELL DONE THE TEAM!**"

"We *did* win ..." Harvey began slowly, "until halftime, anyway. Then Ham complained."

"What about?"

"Mark 1. The ref said he's against the rules. We have to play the game again next week."

"Rot the ref!" said Professor Gertie. "He'll have to change the rules."

"He won't do that," said Harvey.

Professor Gertie sniffed. "Was he good, then?" she asked, watching as Mark 1 practiced with a rolled-up sock.

"Awesome," said Harvey. "Best player I've ever seen. Everyone on our team loved him."

"Oh dear," said Professor Gertie. "That makes it a double waste to feed him to Masher."

"Who?"

"Masher. He chews up old inventions."

Professor Gertie went to her inventing table
and lifted up the tablecloth. Underneath
there was a monstrous machine like a giant
crab. It had black eyes, a large grinning
mouth, grinding teeth and a long, grabbing
arm. Harvey imagined it chewing up Mark 1.
It was horrible.

"You can't feed Mark 1 to Masher!" said
Harvey. "You just can't!"

"I never like mashing my inventions," said
Professor Gertie. "But don't forget, Mark 1 is
only a machine."

"He's not! He's learned to talk. Go on,
Mark 1, say something!"

Mark 1 was busy jumping up to head the
lampshade.

"I have to mash him," said Professor
Gertie. "I don't have any room to keep
inventions that don't work."

"He does work!" said Harvey.

"But the ref won't let him play," said Professor Gertie. "So he's useless."

Mark 1 came over and lifted Harvey into the air. "Stop it!" said Harvey irritably.

"He's showing you how to head the lampshade," said Professor Gertie.

That gave Harvey an idea.

"I know!" he said. "Mark 1 can be our coach. We can practice against him. So he's *not* useless, and he doesn't have to be mashed!"

"Good idea!" said Professor Gertie, suddenly excited again. "And next week you'll need new Bouncing Boots, too. And you could try the Smoke Machine again ..."

"We can't," said Harvey. "The ref said no inventions."

"I don't like that ref! What about Tackle Arms attached to your ankles?"

"No," said Harvey. "The only thing we
need is someone to cheer us on. Nobody
ever does that."

"I could do it!" Professor Gertie opened
her notebook, and started scribbling a new
list. "I'll need a Team scarf..." she muttered.
"And a Team hat... This time, I'm really
going to help The Team win!"

That week, The Team practiced every day. They learned how to get the ball from Mark 1, *and* how to keep it from him.

Darren said, "No one's going to score past me! Watch!"

He threw the ball to Mark 1, and Mark 1 shot at the goal. Darren dove full stretch and saved it.

"Great!" The Team cheered.

"Aw, shucks!" said Mark 1. He ran to get the ball and try again.

"All you have to do is score a goal, Harvey," said Rita. "Then we'll win!"

"Why don't *you* score?" asked Harvey.

"I can't," said Rita, shaking her head. "When I get near the goal my legs turn to jelly. You're our best player, Harvey. *You* have to score!"

That was the real problem, thought Harvey. He had never scored, except in practice. So what chance did he have of scoring against the Ham Soccer Furies? It wasn't Mark 1 who was useless. It was Harvey.

Chapter 5

On Friday, the night before the game, Harvey had a terrible dream.

He dreamed that Masher came looking for him at school, and then chased him home, biting at his ankles. Masher wanted to chew Harvey up, because Harvey was useless.

Harvey ran and ran — then woke up. The sun was shining, and it was just an ordinary Saturday morning …

Harvey looked at the clock. The game! He'd be late!

He pulled on his soccer uniform and ran all the way to the field.

The Ham Soccer Furies were already there.
When their captain saw Harvey, he shouted,
"Where's Trashcan Head? Wouldn't he let
you hold his hand?" The Ham players
exploded with laughter.

The Team huddled close together in a
circle, so no one could hear them whispering.
"You were nearly late!" said Rita. "Where's
Mark 1?"

"He should be here," said Harvey, out of
breath. "Professor Gertie's coming, too. She's
going to cheer us on." He looked around the
field. Where *was* Professor Gertie? She'd
never let him down before. Ever.

Suddenly, there was another roar of
laughter.

"I think she's arrived," said Rita.

Harvey turned to look. "Oh, no!"

Professor Gertie was dressed as a glittering red star. She bounced up and down on Bouncing Sandals. She blew Finger Whistles. She rattled Ankle Bells. And she waved a Clattering Scarf.

The Ham players rolled on the ground, crying with laughter. "Not another *star* player?" their captain asked. "This one's a real super-*star*!"

"Sorry we're late!" Professor Gertie called to Harvey. "It took me ages to get Mark 1 to wear his hat!"

"I'm not surprised," whispered Darren.

Mark 1 was trying to hide behind Professor Gertie. He was wearing a frilly red hat with glittery letters spelling The Team, and his pink-jelly face had turned red with embarrassment.

The ref blew his whistle. Harvey kicked off — straight to a Ham player.

"You're a joke, Harvey!" said the Ham captain. But suddenly the Ham players were quiet, holding their ears.

"The Team! The Team! Come on The Team!"

It was like thunder and an earthquake rolled together.

"What's that?" yelled Darren.

"Professor Gertie's Shouting Mask!" called Harvey.

"It's like having ten thousand fans cheering for us!" said Rita. "She's awesome!"

"Yes," said Harvey. "She is." Professor Gertie didn't always get things right, but she *never* let anyone down.

The Team took the ball and attacked the Ham goal.

"The Team! The Team! Come on The Team!"

The Team were good. Their training had worked, and Ham couldn't get the ball.

Not until Harvey gave it to them.

"Aw, shucks, Harveee!" shouted Mark 1.

Now Ham was attacking. They weren't laughing anymore. They headed straight for Darren's goal.

Suddenly the ball was flying into the top corner, and it was —

"Saved!"

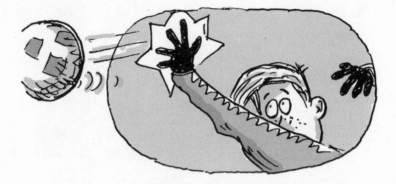

"Told you!" said Darren. "No one scores past me!"

But Ham was now playing better than ever, and Darren had to save shot after shot.

At halftime, it was worse. The Team were
tired, and they had to play defense all the time.

"One minute to go!" called Professor
Gertie, who was biting her Finger Whistles
nervously.

Darren threw the ball to Harvey. Harvey
passed it to Rita, but she passed it straight
back. None of The Team wanted the ball, and
Harvey didn't know what to do. He needed
help. Bouncing Boots or a Smoke Machine or
Tackle Arms …

"Doo itt, Harveeee!"

It was Mark 1, wearing Professor Gertie's Shouting Mask. How come Mark 1 could talk? Nobody had taught him how. He just … did it.

Suddenly, Harvey darted away, dodging past two Ham players. That was it! Harvey didn't need Bouncing Boots or *anything*! He just had to DOO ITT.

"Go on, Harveee!"

Harvey zoomed past the ref, who already had his whistle in his mouth. The game was almost over!

Harvey put on a burst of speed. Whooom! The goal was straight ahead, and he was running out of time! Skid! Swivel! Shoot!

The ball seemed to move in slow motion, like a balloon. The Ham goalie jumped and tried to grab it out of the air, but he missed. Harvey's shot floated gently into the top corner of the net.

"Gooooooaaaalllll!!!"

The ref blew his whistle to end the game. The Team had won!

Mark 1 raced over to Harvey, lifted him onto his shoulders and bounced him around the field.

"M-make h-him s-stop" called Harvey. "I'm g-going t-to b-be s-sick!"

"I can't stop him!" yelled Professor Gertie. "He's re-programmed himself. He pressed his own button *four* times. It makes him celebrate!"

Ham's captain ran over to complain. "No celebrations allowed!" he whined. "It was a lucky goal, that's all."

"That's right!" said the ref, who was angry because he hadn't blown his whistle before Harvey scored. "I'm turning this machine OFF!" He caught Mark 1 and started pressing his button.

"You shouldn't have done that!" said
Professor Gertie.

"Why not?" asked the ref.

"Because you pressed his button five
times. And five times means ..."

Before she could finish, Mark 1 dropped
Harvey, picked up both the ref and the Ham
captain, and ran away with them so no one
could turn him off.

"What does five times do?" Harvey asked Professor Gertie.

"Mark 1's taught himself how to *juggle*!" giggled Professor Gertie. "But don't worry! He'll bring them back when his battery runs out."

"Now we *can* celebrate!" said Harvey. "The Team! The Team! We are The Team!"

And The Team celebrated winning for the first, and best, time ever.

Professor Gertie   Darren   Harvey

Rita   Matt   Steffi   Mark 1

About the Authors

David Bedford was born in Devon, in the southwest of England, in 1969.

David wasn't always a writer – first he was a soccer player! He played for two teams: Appleton Football Club and Sankey Rangers. Although these weren't the worst teams in the league, they never won anything! David was also a scientist. His first job was in the United States, where he worked on discovering new antibiotics.

But, David always loved to read and he decided to start writing stories himself. After a few years, he left his job as a scientist and began writing full time. He now has 10 books published, which have been translated into many languages around the world.

David lives with his wife and daughter in Norfolk, England.

Keith Brumpton has written and illustrated over 35 humorous books for children. He also writes scripts and screenplays. Keith now lives in Glasgow, Scotland.